Garden Path by A Mitchell

Twisted Tales 2015

First published in 2015

by

RAGING AARDVARK PUBLISHING, Dalveen, Australia

Cover Image and Design by A. Mitchell

Peeping Window. Roncesvalles by A. Mitchell

Garden Path by A. Mitchell

ISBN-10: 0-9875331-8-5

ISBN-13: 978-0-9875331-8-0

Twisted Tales 2015

Twisted

Tales

Flash Fiction with a Twist

2015

Edited by Annie Evett and Margie Riley

Raging Aardvark Publishing

Twisted Tales

showcases

the winners of one of the

competitions held celebrating

(Inter)National Flash Fiction Day 2015

Preface

Each year, I am gratified to see flash fiction become more mainstream and accepted as a genre in its own right. Flash Fiction writers share a small but intimate space, where–although characters don't have the opportunity to fully develop–integral writing elements must still be upheld.

Flash fiction is about tight structure, vivid images and focus. The critical skill in writing flash fiction is the ability to convey the message with brevity. There simply isn't the time to entice the reader with atmospheric detail. Sentences need to be fast paced and focused.

The best flash fiction is a complete parcel within its restricted word count. A perfect opening sentence isn't enough to sway readers or judges. The endings needed to leave a question, give a chill or force the reader to read the piece again to pick up the clues they had glossed over. Within a short time, the writers need to get inside the reader's head, have an intellectual and emotional impact. And stop.

Our entrants' stories this year were filled with characters leaping out of the page demanding attention. Some will make you shiver, others give pause to reminisce and pull heart strings, but all will leave an impression.

Enjoy!

Content

Acknowledgements

What a terrible job it was for our judges to choose a dozen tales from the collection of high quality stories they were presented with.

Every year I am struck with gratitude and feel it is an incredible honour to read the submissions which flooded in from around the globe for this year's competition. The support and encouragement received each year fuels our passion to continue and we would like to thank all those involved with the Twisted Tales Project.

It was wonderful to include established writers beside emerging authors, and heart-warming to receive messages from thrilled contributors excited to launch their careers within this anthology.

To this year's judges, Bernadette, Sylvia, Iain, Jon, Ayalla and Patrick, all short story writers and experienced wordsmiths, a huge thank you for your insights, guidance and dedication to uphold quality.

Once again an enormous debt of gratitude to Margie Riley for her editing and proofreading skills, her late night conversations and constant encouragement.

Thank you to Ether Books and the wonderful readers, for your added assistance and enthusiasm in the "People's Choice" selection process.

Without the support and encouragement of Calum Kerr, Director of (Inter)National Flash Fiction Day, this collection would not have reached the audiences and garnered the interest it has.

Most importantly, I'd like to thank family and close friends for their ongoing support and encouragement. Twisted Tales, and all of the creations within Raging Aardvark Publishing, truly would not happen without them.

Annie Evett

Publisher

Margie's Red Pen

What a buzz. Annie's asked (well, sort of—our little joke!) me to help her with the editing of this year's Twisted Tales. Love, love, love it.

As a would-be-if-could-be writer—and yes, I have had a few things published—I know how hard it is to Get It Right. I am in awe of those who manage to make it. Their stories are diverse, interesting, nasty, happy, delicious and delightful. More power to everyone involved.

Editing is, to me, a delight. I am such a word-nerd that I am perfectly happy to go over and over things, read and re-read and then read some more. The comments/suggestions I make come from the heart and I promise my red pen is very pale and lightly applied.

I treat it as an honour to help my friend Annie. She knows how much she means to me. If you didn't know beforehand, let me tell you: she is amazing.

Over The Top

by Guy Bolton

As I rounded the side of the visitors' centre, I knew instantly what had to be done and broke into a desperate sprint across the grass. The middle-aged couple by the path helplessly shouting: "Freddie stop! Keep away from the edge. Please!" The guy in the wheelchair powering across the grass with his strong, muscular, tattooed arms; pumping both wheels as fast as he could, and aimed direct and true towards the cliff-edge ahead.

Even from this distance I could see immediately that he had no legs, and had the appearance of a young soldier. What had happened to him? Probably served overseas, maybe Afghanistan, maybe on the receiving end of some improvised explosives wired across the road. Or a rocket from a carefully concealed long range sniper while out on patrol. Had he lain amid the tattered remains of his pals and colleagues, bloody stumps where his legs had once been, crying out in pain or silently waiting for death to overcome his final, solitary thoughts?

Rescue, helicopter evacuation, hospital, flying home, more hospital, physiotherapy and counselling, rehabilitation—or a close attempt—and home, but never again the same. His face contorted in desperation as he thundered towards the edge. A two hundred foot drop to be smashed on the rocks below.

I had to stop him, but he was quickening his pace as the gravity of the sloping ground pulled him ever closer to the precipice.

With every fibre of my being, I accelerated into a painful burst of speed beyond the limits of my body and managed to gain some ground. I was still several paces behind and the edge was racing up to meet us, a close horizon of green grass just stopping with the distant sea beyond. He was oblivious of my pounding feet behind and with sweat pouring down his strained features just kept careering towards his death. What could have driven him to this? An overwhelming desire to destroy himself in front of the couple I expect were his horrified parents. To have survived such devastating injuries serving your country so the likes of me could sleep safely in my bed at night, and to then feel so empty and betrayed by the world that this was the only way to get out. A final burst with all that you have to go flat-out into oblivion.

I was struggling to keep pace and began to lose ground. I too was gasping and aching throughout my entire frame. My legs felt about to collapse under the sheer momentum of my own driving charge, and my lungs pounded as if they were going to implode with each rasping breath. My eyes were blurred; obscured with sweat and I knew I had to throw all of my remaining energy into a desperate lunge. With a great swing of both arms I pulled all the remaining energy from my legs and threw myself bodily forward at the retreating figure thundering towards the void. And missed.

I fell heavily and rolled over on the grass, instinctively rolling up onto my knees to watch with horror as the squaddie reached the final yard of his young life, and with a heart-stopping crash, he yanked back hard on the tyres, ripping his hands open and somehow flung himself sideways, grabbing the young toddler within feet of the edge. I realised with unbelievable horror that if I had connected with the back of this fearless hero's wheelchair, little Freddie's blood would have been forever on my hands.

VIXEN

BRUSH-PAINTING BY A MITCHELL

Vixen

Simon Sylvester

I nosed between the grit-wet bins of Greenwich, sodium buzzing above, newspapers cartwheeling down the empty road. I shredded bin bags for scraps, and cut my nose on empty tins.

Bill huffed with breath, struggling from his sofa to peer between the curtains.

"There's them bloody foxes in the bins again," he said.

I hummed in agreement, leafed through a magazine without looking, and listened for the clatter of my homeland in the world beyond.

The dog fox found me in Greenwich Park, running wild, scared of people, scared of men. Our nights became a whirligig of scent and taste. In his youth, he was bold and strong; his piss rank against my earth, his teeth between my shoulder blades, nips and yips and dew claws digging deep.

When Bill left for The Trafalgar, I wanted for company. When I was alone, I liked having life about the house. I put cat food in a dish beside the bins. I watched from the window with all the lights turned out, and waited for the foxes.

There were catcalls and cars and dodging between shelters. I crept beneath the boards and slept in the old hospital. I wandered the darkened corridors, and found ghosts still bound to operating beds.

Nights alone, not knowing if he'd come. I don't wear perfume. I need to know the shape of my own scent.

"Billy," I said, "how come you smell of perfume?"

His eyes widened in the dark, reflecting streetlamps, and he didn't say a word. We listened to the foxes in the street. After he'd gone, I clambered to the top of the bin and watched between the windows. I imagined Bill with his Polish barmaid, an eight-limbed something on the sofa. I imagined it was me. I felt the shape of it in my mouth, and tried to make it fit, but it tasted wrong. I slipped, and the bin tumbled over. It spilled a used condom to the path. I scraped my hip on the concrete. My lips rolled back from my teeth.

I haunted parks and ransacked hedgerows, seeking out the blackbird eggs. My snout dripped with yolk. The fragments lay shattered at my feet.

A plate exploded on the wall. Bill laughed and laughed as he held one hand to his head to stem the blood. It welled between his fingers and I tasted copper like a coin upon my tongue. The fragments lay shattered at my feet. I found muddy footprints in the bed, and couldn't remember whose they were.

I licked the scraps from abandoned takeaways. Chips and gravy, sauce and bones. I climbed aboard the bus. No one asked me for a ticket. It was not my country. It was not my land. I slipped in through the cat flap, and robbed the chicken from the table. I curled into a perfect circle on the floor and tucked my nose beneath my tail. I slept for weeks, for months, for years, and woke to the jangle of keys in the door.

For a moment, dreaming in the space between two worlds, it felt like I'd come home.

I picked myself up, and knew myself a vixen. I exhaled and tasted raw, rabbity breath. I took myself upstairs.

Bill slept in his underpants, belly up, white as a soft-boiled egg, soft and ready, the great full moon of it ready for my teeth.

I remember the wet heat of fluid catching in my teeth.

I know it all now, except where the fox comes to a finish, and where the woman starts.

The Bunk Bed Incident

Allan.M Heller

Vladimir Moroz praised his luck at finding an abandoned cabin a few miles outside of Dawson City in the Yukon. The small wooden building was structurally sound, as comfortable as any similar edifice could be in the 30-below weather, and sufficiently isolated from the boisterous mining town. And it presented Moroz with the opportunity to murder another of his fellow prospectors, Anatoly Litvenko.

Most of the would-be miners who flocked to the frigid recesses of northwestern Canada in 1897 had fared poorly, losing their fortunes in search of greater ones, and many, their lives. Moroz had been a successful trapper, but switched vocations when news of the glittering discovery at Bonanza Creek reached his ears. He convinced another trapper, Jacques l'Enfant, to accompany him, as well as two of Moroz's countrymen, Litvenko and Alexander Karpov. The latter had an unfortunate encounter with a Kodiak bear, who mauled Karpov to death after smelling the beef jerky that Moroz had stuffed in his slumbering comrade's coat pockets. Even if his plan had failed, Moroz could have claimed that Karpov had been too drunk to remember hoarding the food.

Now there was one fewer companion with whom to share. The considerable yield that the four had uncovered near El Dorado Creek had prompted them to pack up and head south towards the town of Dyea, where they would take a barge to

Vancouver.

Moroz was a large man, and therefore surprised when Litvenko agreed to let him take the top bunk. L'Enfant bedded on an old cot. Quickly learning that his berth was unsteady, Moroz decided on a risky plan that, if successful, would eliminate a second partner and look like an accident.

An hour after the trio had extinguished the lantern, Moroz shifted his weight back and forth, stopping momentarily upon hearing a loud creak. He waited a few minutes before beginning again. A soft cracking came, then a tremendous snap! Moroz broke into a demonic smile as he plunged five feet and landed with a thunderous boom.

His smile vanished, replaced with a grimace. He heard padded footsteps. Litvenko and L'Enfant stood over him, the former holding the lit lantern. L'Enfant looked horrified; Litvenko, calm.

"I slept on the bearskin rug near the door," he explained to Moroz, who lay immobilized with a shattered spine. "My bunk was uncomfortable." He then added softly in Russian, "Sasha hated beef jerky."

*Originally published online at www.helium.com.

Message Understood

Susan Howe

If I hadn't changed Cassie's bed while she was in the shower, Christmas would have happened as usual. If her phone hadn't rung and I hadn't automatically picked it up and viewed the message, we would have exchanged presents, gorged on chocolate and played daft games, just as we had every other Christmas since she was tiny.

But I had.

There was a moment between ignorance and knowledge as Cassie appeared in the doorway accompanied by cheering football crowds from the TV downstairs, hair wrapped in a towel, her face as white as the sheet in my hand. The definition of her cheekbones startled me. Where had her baby softness gone? And when? I glanced down, blinking back sudden tears.

Something I couldn't make out had appeared on the little screen. Confused, I lifted it closer and turned it round until the image made sense. Stunned, I dropped the phone.

Cassie dived towards it and, unbidden, my foot shot out and pressed it into the carpet. She clawed at my slipper.

"No, Mum. Don't look! Please!"

I pushed her away and she fell against the chest of drawers we had decoupaged together, her eyes wide. As I bent to retrieve the phone, she lunged for my arm, tugging at my sleeve and whimpering. I held her off with my elbow while I transferred it to my other hand and scrolled through the messages with trembling fingers, back to the first. There were no words, just a close-up photograph of an eye, blurred and unrecognisable.

The next picture was unmistakably Cassie's ear, one of her birthday earrings flashing in the light. The next, a man's thumb; the next, a slender wrist. Alternate body parts switched from smooth and pale to rough and hairy, each more disturbing than the last as they crept towards areas not normally exposed.

Cassie let me go and slumped to the floor, hiding her face as she drew long, shuddering breaths.

The final few shots stole the last of my strength and I sank down on the bed, closing my eyes but unable to halt the procession of images that flickered by.

"I'm sorry, Mummy."

Her stammered words echoed the past, when a scared little girl had torn my best dress while pretending to be me. I forced myself to look at my daughter and that same terrified child stared back.

"But why?" I managed.

"I don't know," she said. "It started as a silly game. I didn't mean—"

I searched her face. "Who is it, Cassie?"

Her tearful gaze sharpened briefly. She hesitated, then

turned away.

"No one you know."

She reached for the phone and I almost gave it back but, as I weighed it in my hand, a shadow lurking at the back of my mind sidled forwards and took shape. Heart thudding, I scrolled to Cassie's last message and hit Send. Our eyes locked.

From the other end of the house, the familiar notes of her stepfather's ringtone penetrated the silence.

What's a Mother to Do?

Tina Pisco

We huddle together at the top of the ridge, our sweat pungent in the dark. Below us the camp is quiet. A man's snore breaks the silence. It makes me want to puke, but it's better than the screams we heard earlier as we crouched behind the rocks. They were sharp and shrill until they became muffled, as if someone had clamped a strong hand over the screeching mouth. As night fell we heard sobbing coming from the pen where the girls are chained together. Then a gruff voice had yelled, and the crying had stopped.

There are only five of us left. We set out when we heard that they had taken our daughters. Our husbands and parents begged us not to go, but our rage made us deaf to their pleas as we strapped on our weapons: guns, knives, dynamite. Anything we could find. We picked up more along the way. This war is so wasteful of weapons and women. We found a rocket launcher in the hollow of a tree. We found a girl's broken body covered in blood and flies. We were relieved that we did not recognize her.

It was months before we found the camp. They'll all be pregnant by now.

The men are strong and many. Our rage is stronger. We cannot win, but we will not be defeated. Rachel creeps back up the ridge on her belly, a silent, slithering shadow. She has placed the dynamite around the pen so that it will be quick.

She says that it was too dark to see them. I know that she didn't want to look.

I caress the rocket launcher and pray that my aim is true. I picture our daughters sleeping; their sweet, little girl, sleepy smell. I blow a kiss in their direction, imagine hugging them, stroking their hair, watching them giggle and laugh. I pull the trigger, sending them to heaven; the men to hell.

The New Thieves

Thaisa Frank

One night my lover said: You must learn to be like one of the new thieves—they never steal, they add. They enter rooms without force and leave hairpins, envelopes, roses. Later they leave larger things like pianos; no one ever notices. You must learn to be like that woman in the bar who dropped her glove so softly I put it on. You must learn to be like that man who offered his wife so gently I thought we'd been married for seventeen years. You must learn to fill me with riches—so quietly I'll never notice. After saying this he draped himself in all my scarves and lay back in bed. What can I give you? I said, what do you really want? Nothing I can tell you about, he said.

The next day I brought home a woman in camouflage, and placed her on top of our bed. She looked just like me and talked just like me and that night while I pretended to sleep, she made love to my lover. I thought I'd accomplished my mission, but as soon as she left, he said to me: I knew she wasn't you. I knew by the way she'd kissed.

I tried other things, but nothing eluded him—new shoes just like his old ones, scuffed in the same places, keepsakes from his mother, books he'd already read. He recognized everything and threw it away.

One rainy fall afternoon when I couldn't think of anything

else to give him, I went into an elegant bar, the kind with leather chairs and soft lights. I ordered a glass of chilled white wine, and suddenly, without guile, there was an instant understanding between me and the bartender. That night while my lover slept next to us, he and I made love, and the next morning he hung up his clothes in my lover's closet. Soon he moved in with us, walking like a cat, filling our rooms with objects. My lover never noticed, and now at night he lies next to us, thinking that he's the bartender. He breathes his air, dreams his dreams and in the morning when we all wake up, he tells me that he's happy.

Debut

Therese Edmonds

The microphone crackles slightly as she speaks into it. It rattles her; she'd thought the quality would be much better. Her voice is more confident than she'd expected too, and is the larger of the two surprises. She fights off a little giggle of nerves. Through the glare of the lights she can just make out her audience, dim shapes and her so vivid, alone in that pool of light. She feels like a giant, towering so high above them. He hadn't prepared her for that, for looking down on them with nowhere to hide. It's so foreign to her. She holds her eye contact. And smiles.

She can't see him but she knows he's there—the man who'd trained her, standing just out of sight, watching her debut. She has a sudden image of him mouthing the words and has to push her stomach back down by tensing her abdomen and breathing out hard and steady through her nose. Her smile doesn't break, and she's proud of that. She hadn't managed it in her training, not even once.

The in-between world, stretching after her opening remark, gives her time enough to think on all that led to it, to being here. She'd come to it startled, only stepping onto this platform because he'd seen something in her. She thought she'd be paying her dues for years. There were a lot of people ahead of her, more experienced, better at it. He'd told the story so many times of how funny the look on her face was when he first suggested it. How did he know? What was it that he saw, does it have a name?

It amazes her how effortless it all seems, now she's here—doing it, actually doing it. She'll look for it now, she'll find a name for it and she'll look for it in the ones who'll be learning from her. And then suddenly there it is, the sound she'd been told about, that he'd drilled into her until her reaction was faultless: her audience had responded. She leans into the mic again, this time so comfortable and in control.

"Would you like any drinks or fries with that?"

She smiles, her future suddenly so certain.

Friday Roses

Cath Bore

The red roses Brian sends on Fridays are delivered to the house, bound in a tight bundle. The taut rubber band pinks my fingers and thorny stems, long and tentacular, splice my skin as I unpick the stubborn brown rubber. My fingers cut and bleed, but push the flowers into a vase.

"Have they arrived, the flowers?" Brian rings up and asks, as always. He can't wait. It's too urgent. He needs to know, now.

"Yes, they've arrived."

He pauses.

"Thank you," I say. I wait for the next question, my answer ready. I have the words, right here.

"And do you like them?"

"I love them."

He makes me say it every week, every Friday, forces me to lie. Three words, three syllables, I squeeze them out on cue. I love them, I love you.

I'm a liar, and sometimes I think he knows. I hate the roses more than I despise him. The flowers offer up no scent, shiny

plastic petals scratch the end of my nose as he forces me to sniff them and inhale plain air that smells of tap water.
Flowers every week, how romantic, delivered to your door, each Friday. You're so lucky.

"Yes," I smile. "I'm lucky."

My cracked ribs creak as I force uncomfortable words out from lips stiff and awkward with lies.

In the end, all it takes is a little push. I watch Brian fall down the stairs, arms in frantic circles, hands grabbing air, gob flapping silently. He can't believe my cheek, nor can I. Brian's words of protest are snatched from his mouth, air solidified in his lungs.

I taste copper and smell its perfume, realise I've bitten my tongue and hold it between my teeth as he windmills downwards, legs pedalling. He hits the ground. He breaks.
Relief washes through me like a flood but the police believe my tears. They're embarrassed during the interview, apologise for all the questions, say sorry over and over. I nod that it's okay. Because it is okay; everything is, now.

The following Friday, roses arrive as usual, red like blood.

Elevation

Vesna McMaster

Don't die before me. 8th April 2013

You do a double-take. Not what you'd expect to find on a hot photocopier on a Tuesday morning in the Tokyo headquarters of a soft drinks company.

You look around, paper still in hand. Everyone is eyes-down busy. A few people moving about at the back of the open-plan expanse of sleek black heads but they don't display any characteristics of having recently used a copier.

Something moves at your elbow and makes you jump. The secretary from Purchasing, the one who always wears black tights and pleated mid-thigh skirts no matter what the weather, with a stack of papers, standing, blinking, waiting. You slip the note into your file, copy your single sheet and leave with a little bow.

At your desk you take the note out again. It's peculiar because the original sheet was a lined foolscap, but the writing is printed from a computer. Not only that but just where the writing is there's a pattern underneath and the lines are hidden. It's a Hello Kitty. Hello Kitty ticker-tape with "Don't die before me" typed over it.

At lunchtime you pick up your handbag. Your pantyhose have run at the top but no-one can see it yet. If you're quick you can get a new pair at the department store across the road, pick up a lime-coconut yogurt shake for lunch and email your mum with the pictures from last night's visit to your sister's before break finishes. Pity you don't have time to get some new shoes, these ones need re-heeling at the least, left heel's catching on the carpet.

Mr Matsumoto glances up at you as you pass and smiles. You smile and nod back. He always reminds you of a sweet-bean roll: rounded and pale, sweet and soft and vaguely reminiscent of childhood. Maybe because he looks a bit like your uncle who lives in the country and whose house smells of charcoal smoke and the wind blowing in from the mountains.

"How are you today?" you say, not quite stopping.

His expression increases into a grin. "It's my birthday!"

You have to stop now. "Oh! Happy birthday. Congratulations, I didn't know!"

He's nodding. "Yes, yes. My youngest daughter gave me a card. Made it herself." He lifts the item off his table: a crayon drawing of a person, a rainbow, some flowers. You breathe approval, but the breath stops when you notice the decoration along the bottom edge.

Hello Kitty ticker tape.

Mr Matsumoto still smiles and nods. His hair needs a cut and the duffle bag under his desk is ajar showing jumbled gym clothes. You mumble incoherent politeness and clutch your handbag shopwards.

You stop at the bathroom and when you get to the elevator Mr Matsumoto is also waiting there. He stands quiet, eyes up at the floor indicator, hands clasped neat in front. He notices you, raises eyebrows smiling, does a tiny bow. You tap down the corridor towards him. The elevator pings. The door opens, he turns once more looking over his shoulder, bowing, and steps in.

There's a two second silence, and a hideous thud.

You run forward. Gasp at the elevator opening, clutching at the metal.

There's no carriage. Just an empty shaft, dropping down into the darkness. You propel yourself backwards.

There's no-one in the corridor. The twin elevator opens with an empty Ping, this time with the carriage. You reel away.

Level 18, level 15, 8, 5. You fly down the staircase, heels making an uneven Tap Clop Tap Clop Tap Clop every step to your flawed shoes. In the lobby a small crowd of black and grey clad workers waits at the closed elevator door, pressing the buttons, mildly annoyed. You do not want to see the broken body of Mr Matsumoto when that door opens any second. You run out of the building, handbag trailing.

Pantyhose. A yogurt shake. Everything's going to be all right.

The blare of the truck, the shiny, pristine metal of the grill and bull-bar as it slides towards you from the left. The last thing you see.

Dedicated to the memory of Jany Gräf, who provided the prompt for this story.

Bianca

Gwen Hart

On the way to the hospital, I balanced a potted gerbera daisy between my knees while my mother recited the rules for interacting with Bianca.

"You have to keep her spirits up," she said. "You mustn't cry."

"I won't," I promised, my toes twitching excitedly. It had been a few months since my mother had forbidden me from seeing Bianca after school, proclaiming her a "bad influence."

"They probably have board games and playing cards," continued my mother. She fixed me with a look. "Let Bianca win," she said.

Because Bianca was bird-boned and delicate as a china doll, people always assumed she was younger than me, but we were both ten years old. Bianca always had the best ideas. She'd gotten the secret telephone company test numbers, and we'd made the phone in her mother's dress shop ring at inopportune times one whole Saturday. And she'd had me put more and more toilet paper into the toilet in the girls' lavatory while she flushed and flushed until the toilet exploded into a whitewater volcano.

"If Bianca jumped off a cliff, would you jump, too?" my

mother demanded when we got into trouble for the third time in a month. Secretly I thought that if Bianca jumped off of a cliff, she would probably fly.

***

As we approached Bianca's room, a doctor strode away from us, white coat flapping. I held my breath, but when I peeked around my mother, Bianca turned her head on the pillow and smiled at me. She was pale, but her blue eyes still sparkled.

"You two have fun," said my mother as she left to have coffee with Bianca's mother.

"I brought you this gerbera daisy," I said, holding out the pot.

Bianca wrinkled her nose. "Put that on the table, you goose," she said.

I placed the flowerpot next to a great bouquet of yellow roses with baby's breath.

"Why everyone thinks you want to look at a bunch of old flowers just because you're dying is beyond me," she said.

"But, Bianca," I said, trying desperately to think of something encouraging to say.

"Braid my hair," she whispered, her fingers on my arm as light as feathers.

Obediently, I separated her blonde curls carefully between my thick fingers.

"First my foot gave out from under me, and then I got so weak I couldn't even turn over in bed," she said breathlessly.

"They took oodles of blood and made me pee in a pot." She pulled up the sleeve of her nightgown and showed me a series of bruises. "And they won't say what's wrong with me, but Reverend Tom came and talked with me."

Then Bianca described heaven, how Reverend Tom had said she could walk on the clouds, and everyone would be there to greet her: her grandparents, her dog Barney, even her father, whom she'd never met since he was killed in the war. She wouldn't have to spend any more time in hospitals, no more blood draws or long, boring, bed-ridden afternoons.

I tucked up the ends of the braid.

"Use the baby's breath," she said.

I took some sprigs from the vase and carefully inserted them over her temples.

"It's perfect," she said, admiring herself in the mirror.

"Now I need you to do something else for me, Mary," she said.

Bianca had it all worked out, and when I followed her instructions, it was surprisingly easy. It only took a few minutes.

I fluffed the pillow and put it back under her head, swept away a few crushed pieces of baby's breath, and replaced them with new stems. I straightened out the blanket so she was perfectly tucked in.

Then, just as she'd instructed me, I whipped up some tears and ran out into the hallway wailing.

***

My mother was obviously shaken. Her fingers fluttered on

the steering wheel. I wanted tell her the secret—how I'd helped Bianca get to heaven just a tiny bit ahead of schedule. I smiled inside, picturing Bianca dancing on a cloud.

"I suppose it's a blessing you were with her," my mother said, "but if I'd known this would happen, I wouldn't have left you alone with her." She shook her head. "And to think, the doctor had just told them Bianca was going to make a full recovery!"

The Cabin

Miranda Kate

With each mile he drove Gary felt his shoulders loosen. He watched the dusk come in as the land opened up, the clouds reflecting the last few rays of the day, colouring them a rusty orange. They reminded him to pull off for wood at a gas station before he reached the cabin tonight. He wanted to get a good fire going as soon as he arrived.

He needed this weekend. He'd been holding on for a long time. City life took more than it should—especially since he'd started dating Melinda.

He'd met her at the office. All his colleagues had been hot for her, but she'd only had eyes for him—and what eyes they were! He ended up being unable to resist. He wished he had.

She'd used all her wiles on him, although they hadn't been necessary. She'd sidle up to him at the coffee machine and say, "Hey Gary, how you doing today?"

And he'd try not to choke on his coffee while replying coolly, "Good, Melinda."

He'd been told before that he was a magnet for women, but he didn't see it. He thought he was too big, too clumsy, and too quiet. But they seemed to like him; they'd come and chat to him about their lives and he would listen, trying to understand as best he could. He'd been a city boy all his life, but he still struggled to relate to city folk. They were all so busy with so much stuff that wasn't important. He didn't get it.

It was why he'd bought the cabin, his place of refuge, of peace, but he didn't get there as often as he'd like. His dream was to move there permanently, but city life was costly—and not just financially. Melinda had taught him that.

It had been so easy in the beginning; their first couple of dates a delight, and on the third they'd spent the night together. He'd been bowled over by how incredible she was, and although he wanted to keep it quiet at work, she'd had other ideas. By morning break the following day everybody had known. The guys wanted the low down and the girls complimented him on details they shouldn't have known about. They were considered a hard and fast couple straight away, no longer two individuals who were dating. Gary struggled with that. He wanted to keep work and home life separate, but she didn't care.

Initially he found peace in his own apartment, but then she started to invade that too. More and more often she'd turn up unannounced, standing there in the doorway batting her eyelids at him and he'd relent. He couldn't refuse her. They'd spend days in bed, or watching telly, occasionally taking walks in the park—whatever she wanted, because he couldn't say no to her. Until one day he noticed how much stuff she'd left behind in his flat.

He went looking for a sweater in a bottom drawer and found she'd moved some of his clothes to make room for hers. Then he spotted her 'spare' make-up bag on the chest of drawers, her 'spare' toothbrush in the bathroom, and her music CDs stacked up on top of his in the lounge. He wasn't ready for that. It wasn't what he wanted. He needed his space. That was when he knew it was time to go up to the cabin.

He'd thought about taking her there a couple of times, but had held back. He'd never mentioned it. He was glad he hadn't.

The lights of a gas station ahead brought him out of his thoughts and he pulled in, spotting the stacks of firewood outside. He grabbed a few, along with a bag of coals and went inside to pay. He exchanged pleasantries with the owner, reassuring him he'd be fine loading them up himself as he went back out to the car.

Opening the trunk, he tucked the bundles in around her. He took a brief moment to touch her cold face, wishing things could have turned out differently. If only she'd known what boundaries she was crossing.

Dave

Keith Gillison

"Hello Dave, I'm Adam. Let's have some fun."

They were the first words the eighteen-year-old Adam ever said to Dave and were forever etched in his memory. When he thought of those words it always gave him a warm feeling inside, and took him back to the happiest day of his life. Up until that point nobody had ever shown much interest in Dave.

All that changed when Adam came along. Suddenly Dave felt needed, he felt loved. The two quickly became inseparable. They went shopping together, cruised the streets together trying to look cool and visited garages together to look at the shiny new models.

"What a beauty, eh?" Adam would say. Dave didn't agree.

Sometimes they went to the beach and just sat there listening to the noise of the waves crashing against the sand. Adam never went anywhere without Dave. He told him his secrets and all about the big noise he was going to make with his life. Dave listened. They were happy days, special times—the two amigos taking on the world.

Then it changed. Dave got sick. His deep, hacking cough made it difficult for him to keep up with Adam. As Dave's insides decayed and he got sicker, Adam grew angry. When he wanted to go for a meal or to the cinema, Dave was too sick to come. He was too sick to go anywhere. Adam's friendly conversation had disappeared; when he spoke to Dave now it was through gritted teeth. Pretty soon Adam stopped visiting him altogether. He had places to go, people to see. Dave was holding him back.

Time passed. Dave's health didn't improve. It was a miserable time for him; all he could do was remember the happy times he had spent with Adam and hold onto the hope that one day his friend would come back to him.

The day arrived. Dave knew it would. Adam was in high spirits, chatting away to him the way he used to in the good old days. Dave hadn't been out for a long time because of his health so, when Adam promised him a trip somewhere special he felt better already. When they arrived at their destination, it wasn't somewhere Dave recognised. There was a sadness in Adam's voice as he spoke to him.

"Goodbye Dave. Thanks for everything." Then Adam disappeared.

Not goodbye, thought Dave, never goodbye. We have our ups and downs but we always get through it.

As the metallic teeth of the crane's rusty mouth crushed through Dave's skull, his final thoughts were of his best friend Adam and all the wonderful times they had spent together.

Adam ran his hand along the gleaming black bonnet of the new Volkswagen Golf before he unlocked the door and sat in the driver's seat. He turned the key in the ignition, pressed the accelerator to the floor and grinned as the engine roared into life.

"Hello Steve," he said "I'm Adam. Let's have some fun."

Counting to Paradise

Tina Pisco

He imagines them in his bed, counts them one by one; adds names to the number: Kadiza, Shamima, Amira. Running out of local names, he turns to Hollywood: Angelina, Kate, Emma. He knows their every curve, their hidden smiles. As he counts he feels himself stiffen, drops his left hand (using the right is haraam), first slowly, slowly, then faster, faster, until the night explodes, and he falls asleep.

At first he never made it past eleven. In time he learns to hold back; counts to fifteen, then twenty. The houris dance around him in a swirl of soft skin. Their dangling breasts swing as their hips sway to the rhythm of his breathing. The numbers and names, curves and smiles, breasts and hips become a frenzy of flesh, like sharks feeding off him.

When he masters seventy-two he will be ready. He will go to the market. He will pull the wire. The world will explode and he will sleep in their arms forever.

Biographies

Cath Bore is a writer of fiction and fact, published in the UK and US. Her flash fiction can be found in National Flash Fiction Day anthologies 2014 and 2015, Flash Fiction Magazine and the first Two Slim Volume books (Pankhearst Publishing, 2015). She writes Obsessive Pop Culture Disorder, the fortnightly column for Liverpool's The Guide.

Based on Merseyside UK, she has an MA in Creative Writing from Liverpool John Moores University. Cath is currently completing a crime novel.

Website: https://cathbore.wordpress.com/

Therese Edmonds's diverse works include stand-up comedy, short stories and films, monologues, business documents, eulogies, television interviews, comedy skits, copywriting and a pantomime for sea lions. She's won three prizes in Western Australia's Maj Monologues, was shortlisted for ScreenWest's new writer's award and is counted among Wendy Harmer's 'Australia's Funny Women'.

Annie Evett is a prolific scribbler of characters, weaver of storylines, champion of the short story, professional cat herder, wielder of a balanced editing razor while beating recalcitrant words into shape. She is a contributing editor in a number of publications and manages a small indie publishing

house committed to promoting the short story form. She tweets @AnnieEvett, is Linkedin and can be stalked on http://annieevett.com

Thaisa Frank has published six books, including a novel, *Heidegger's Glasses* (2010, translated into ten languages) and *Enchantment* (2012 - short stories). She has received two PEN awards and is a three-time nominee for a Pushcart Prize.

Keith Gillison is a writer of flash fiction, short stories and novels in many genres including humour, crime and horror. His stories have been published in magazines and online.

His first novel, *The Boss Killers*—a dark crime comedy—was published in 2015.

Gwen Hart teaches writing at Buena Vista University in Storm Lake, Iowa. Her poetry and fiction have appeared in literary journals such as *Prism International,* *Calliope,* and *Measure.* Her poetry collection, *Lost and Found,* is available from David Robert Books.

Allan M. Heller is the author of five non-fiction books, most recently Graveyards of Montgomery County, Pennsylvania. He is a published poet and short fiction writer, and in February 2014 was

appointed poet laureate of Hatboro, Pennsylvania. He lives with his wife, Tatiana, and their cat, Rocky.

Susan Howe writes short fiction and has won several prizes over recent years. Her longer stories can be found on Ether Books, at Alfie Dog Fiction, and in numerous anthologies and magazines. A selecting editor for FlashFlood, Susan lives in rural Herefordshire and occasionally blogs at http://howesue.wordpress.com

Miranda Kate is a British expat living in Holland, who by day is a freelance editor, and by night a writer. Primarily a novel writer, Miranda enjoys exploring her writing through flash fiction, finding a certain satisfaction in the end result. You can read more on her blog, Finding Clarity on www.purplequeennl.blogspot.nl

Vesna McMaster writes mystery novels under the pen name of Moosey and short stories in her own. Her bio is 'complicated' but like all Moose she likes her fiction served straight up, with a twist. www.MooseysMysteries.Weebly.Com   & www.VesnaMcMaster.Com

A Mitchell wields a mean 6 HB pencil infusing her eclectic artwork with years of teaching, traversing the corporate landscape and motherhood.

An emerging artist and photographer, she has had a number of prints, brush painting and sketches published. Follow her on Facebook https://www.facebook.com/AMitchellArtist

Tina Pisco has been a professional writer for over twenty years. She has published novels, non-fiction and poetry. She lives in West Cork, Ireland. Her first collection of short stories will be published by Fish Publishing in 2016, twenty years after Fish published her first short story.

Margie Riley's been a bibliophile forever and knows that writing is a complicated game. Published in Ether Books, Stringybark's *Behind the Wattles* and *No Tea Tomorrow*, and the national newspaper, The Australia, she's contributed to various online writers' mags and is an inveterate commentator. She belongs to a book club (doesn't

everybody?) and a writers' group. She uses her status as an elder to justify her gentle wielding of the editor's red pen. Caducity hasn't quite set in—yet. She can be found here www.bettermanuscriptediting.com.au, and on Facebook.

Simon Sylvester is a writer, teacher and occasional filmmaker. He has written more than 1,000 flash stories on Twitter, and his debut novel *The Visitors* was published by Quercus in 2014, going on to win the Book Box and Not The Booker prizes.

Our Judges

No competition, especially an international one such as Twisted Tales, could gather the support, respect and following it enjoys, without an incredible team behind it. Our judges each year are drawn from experienced editors and writers with an expansive knowledge in both the publishing and writing fields.

The Anthology is in its 4th year and has attracted hundreds of entries along with a panel of esteemed judges, who volunteer their time and expertise to mark the entries and choose the top 13.

It's an extremely difficult job as stories are of high quality with many respected and published authors entering along side emerging writers.

As a small gesture of thanks, we recognise their expertise here.

 **Bernadette Russell** is a writer and performer based in London, UK. She's been co-running the short story variety night "Are You Sitting Comfortably?" with Gareth Brierley and their company White Rabbit since 2008. She has created storytelling shows for National Theatre, Southbank Centre, and the Queen's Diamond Jubilee amongst many others, including the work of 100s of short story writers as well as three magicians, two dogs and a snake charmer.

Her children's book *Do Nice Be Kind Spread Happy* is out now, the next *Be The Change Make it Happen* is due out Feb 2016. Her adult short stories are published by Pulp Press and Ether. At the moment she is writing about superheroes and touring a show to people's bedrooms, although these two things are not connected.

Check out her on the website www.thewhiterabbit.org.uk

Iain Maloney was born in Aberdeen, Scotland and now lives in Japan. In 2013 he was shortlisted for the Dundee International Book Prize. His debut novel First Time Solo was shortlisted for the 2014 Guardian Not The Booker Prize. His second novel *Silma Hill* is out now.

Jonathan Cardew is a writer and editor living in Milwaukee. His short fiction appears in Atticus Review, Segue, Flash: The International Short-Short Story Magazine, Every Day Fiction, and elsewhere. He edits The Phoenix Literary

Magazine at Milwaukee Area Technical College.

Ayalla Buckanan is a poet and author. A poem about her psychotic cat, Norman Bates, was in Purrfect Poetry and short fiction *No Choice But Chosen* was in Short Story Sunday. She lives in New Zealand with her cats, the aforementioned Norman Bates and Tesla the genius kitten, and a crazy rabbit named Straightjacket.

Patrick Harkin was first published in 2012 with *Not That I'm Bitter* and has gone on to show he's really not bitter, honest, with other stories.

He judged for Ether's 2013 *Journeys* competition and Raging Aardvarks 2014 Flash Fiction Anthology, *Twisted Tales*.

Sylvia Petter is an Australian based in Vienna who writes short, long, serious and fun. She has a PhD in Creative Writing and has published the collections, *The Past Present* (2001), *Back Burning* (2007), *Mercury Blobs* (2013), and writing as AstridL, *Consuming the Muse – erotic tales* (2013). A German translation of several of her  stories was published in 2014 as *Geflimmer der Vergangenheit*. Sylvia was Co-Director Vienna for the 14th International Conference on the Short Story in English in 2014. She has led flash fiction workshops in Switzerland, France and Vienna, Austria. More at www.sylviapetter.com

About the Publisher

Raging Aardvark Publications is an Australian indie publisher which promotes creative artists of edgy, off-kilter work in anthologies of short stories, flash fiction and poetry, as well as delving into non-fiction.

They are committed to sourcing a wide range of cross-genre fiction which not only pushes boundaries, but also stirs the emotions of readers.

Non-fiction themes explore living an authentic life, balancing the challenges of the 21st Century and exploring the vast range of experiences within relationships.

Raging Aardvark supports International Flash Fiction Day through an extensive competition culminating in the anthology "Twisted Tales".

As their literary imprint, Cats With Thumbs, they produce a blogzine biannually with a collected anthology of favourite poetry, short stories, artwork and photography; published in July.

Titles available from Amazon include:

Choose your Adventures—written by a number of authors

History's Keeper

Dust and Death

Zombie Now

Anthologies involving a number of authors

New Sun Rising—Stories for Japan

Twisted Tales 2012—Flash Fiction with a Twist

Twisted Tales 2013—Flash Fiction with a Twist

Twisted Tales 2014—Flash Fiction with a Twist

Twisted Tales 2015—Flash Fiction with a Twist

Cats With Thumbs 2015

Single author anthologies

Consuming the Muse—erotic tales—AstridL

Mercury Blobs—Sylvia Petter

Love Just Is—Kate Murray

Shadows Close—Kate Murray

Sandman—Simon Humphreys

Non Fiction

Reclaim—Sex after Birth—Annie Evett

It's up to Me—Warren Hooke

Upcoming Titles

Raunchy Recipes—Erotic tales blended with a recipe—Anthology

Anthology—Sartres' Lonely Toybox—Annie Evett

Brother Dragon and Racoon walk the Camino—Annie Evett

Letters to Saffy—Kiki Jarrott

For more information, check their website.

http://ragingaardvark.com

www.ingramcontent.com/pod-product-compliance
Lightning Source LLC
Chambersburg PA
CBHW020646130626
46552CB00003B/1421